Let's Draw!

Action
and Animation

Leon Baxter

IDEALS CHILDREN'S BOOKS
Nashville, Tennessee

in association with

 Belitha Press

Let's draw together . . .

In the first six *Let's Draw!* books, you discovered the basic principles of line, color, movement, shape, and proportion. If you have tried all those ideas, you should now be feeling more confident about drawing pictures.

In these new books I am encouraging you to be observant and inventive so that you will enjoy drawing even more. You can learn how to compose and construct your pictures, how to create space and movement, and even how to have three-dimensional fun with paper itself.

Don't use a ruler. Draw all straight lines freehand. This is a good exercise for getting your eyes and hands to work together. Try out some of these ideas. Use your imagination and see your paper come to life.

Things you will need:

colored pencils	paint	glue
crayons	construction paper	brushes
pastels	lots of drawing paper (white and colored)	scissors
markers		

Have a good time!

Leon Baxter

First published in U.S. 1989 by Ideals Publishing Corp., Nashville, Tennessee
in association with Belitha Press Limited,
31 Newington Green, London N16 9PU
Text and illustrations in this format copyright © Belitha Press 1989
Text and illustrations copyright © Leon Baxter
Art Director: Treld Bicknell   Editor: Carol Watson
ISBN 0-8249-8329-7
Typesetting by Chambers Wallace, London
Printed in Italy for Imago Publishing

Action!

Here is a picture sequence.
It tells an action story.

The action is shown by bending and stretching lines and by
drawing something about to happen or that has happened.
This gives the suggestion of time.

Let's begin by looking at how we move.

How do we walk?

To keep your balance, you swing your arms in the opposite direction to your legs. Like this:

He's right.

Can you draw a boy walking?

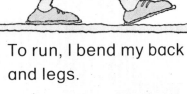

To run, I bend my back and legs.

Now draw him running.

4

The race

This boy is doing exercises.

bending

stretching

 Running in place

Can you draw a girl doing the same exercises?

Now draw the other athletes in the race.

How to suggest time

In these three pictures we can show:

before	during	after

1. He is going to kick the ball.

2. He is kicking the ball.

3. He has kicked the ball.

Now draw someone kicking the ball.

1. before	2. during	3. after

before	during	after
1. She is going to throw the ball.	2. She is throwing the ball.	3. She has thrown the ball.

Draw a tennis player about to hit the ball.

1. before	2. during	3. after

7

Action sequences

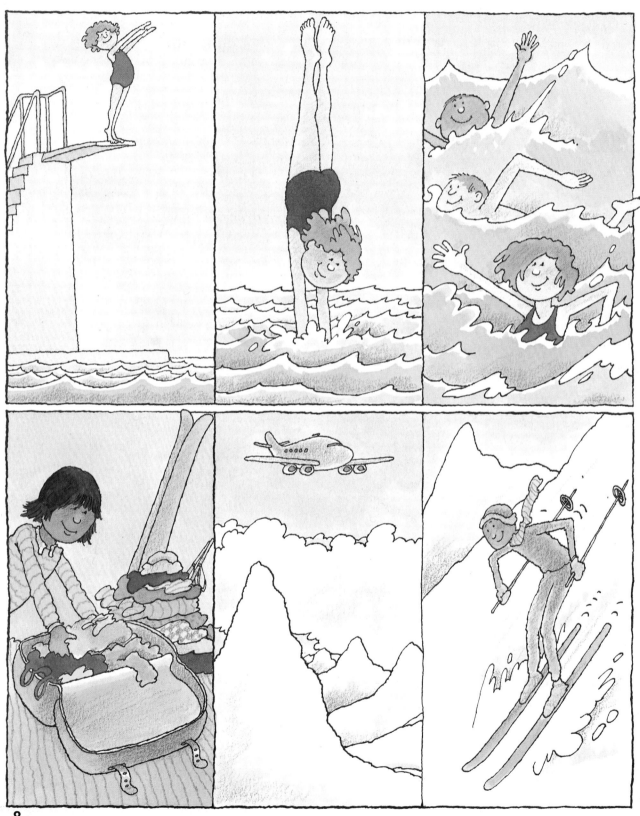

Here are two sequences showing people enjoying a vacation. One sequence of actions takes place in a very short space of time, while the other takes place over a much longer period. Some actions are all over in seconds, others fill days or weeks. By changing the backgrounds, showing travel and a change of climate, you can suggest the passage of time.

Choose summer or winter and make a vacation picture. Draw all the things you like to do.

Make the wind blow

The wind is blowing this way: ←

Draw a flag flying this way: →

Draw a tree with the wind blowing this way: ←

Draw laundry on a clothesline dancing in the wind.
The wind is blowing this way: →

10

This boy is going for a walk.

Drawing a strong breeze will help him on his way.

Draw a storm with the boy hurrying home.

These planes are giving an aerobatic display.

Draw your own planes – make them dive, climb, and roll.

Helicopters put their tails up when they take off.

Draw a helicopter taking off.

Sailboats lean over as they zip along.

Draw a boat sailing in a strong wind.

Motorcycles can jump.

Draw a motorcycle jumping a ditch.

Moviemaking

These men are filming a stuntman driving a car over a cliff.

Draw your favorite action scene in these four frames.

These quarrymen are using high explosives to blast rock from a cliff face.

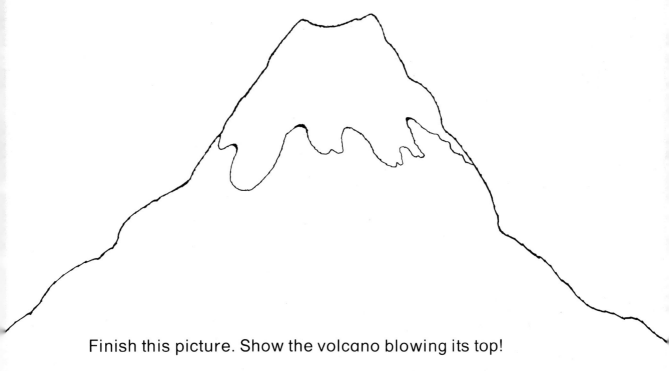

Finish this picture. Show the volcano blowing its top!

Fun at the fair

There is lots of action at the fair.
Finish this big picture.

Mini-movies

You can make your own movies by using a paper cylinder that spins on the turntable of a record player set at 45 rpm. The movie is drawn on a paper strip placed inside the cylinder.
You watch through slits cut in the cylinder.

To make a 12-frame cartoon movie you will need:

1. A strip of stiff paper or poster board 20 in. × 6 in. which is black on one side and white on the other.

2. A strip of paper $19\frac{1}{4}$ in. × $2\frac{3}{4}$ in. for the movie strip.

3. A pencil, ruler, pair of scissors, black marker, paste, 2 paper clips, and a record player.

Making the cylinder

The cylinder is made from a strip of stiff paper or poster board. If you cannot buy black and white paper or poster board, color one side of the strip with a black marker. (Paint, crayons, or pastels are too messy.) There are twelve slits – draw them onto the strip and carefully cut them out. All measurements are shown below.

extra $\frac{5}{8}$ in. overlap for pasting

Now paste the two ends of the strip together with a $\frac{5}{8}$ in. overlap.
The **black** surface should be on the outside.

Use the paper clips to hold the surfaces together while the paste dries.

Turn to the next page for drawing the movie.

Drawing the movie

Draw or trace the 12 pictures on the opposite page onto the strip of paper ($19\frac{1}{4}$ in. × $2\frac{3}{4}$ in.). Use a black marker to color the man in.

Showing the movie

Keeping the picture on the *inside*, bring the two ends of the movie strip together and place it inside the cylinder, like this:

Place the cylinder onto the turntable of your record player – making sure it is centered. Now switch on. Look through the slits and watch your man
doing headstands! Use the same cylinder to make your own movies.

Note that the action runs backwards from right to left.

A paper strip $19\frac{1}{4}$ in. × $2\frac{3}{4}$ in. divides into 12 frames, each $1^9/_{16}$ in. wide. Draw your picture in each frame like this.

Keep it simple – experiment with color and all kinds of action.

1   2   3   4

5   6   7   8

9   10   11   12

What happened?

Here are the beginning and end of the story.
Can you draw what happened in between?